Storm on Snowbelle Mountain

Read more
UNICORN DIARIES
books!

Unicorn Diaries

Storm on Snowbelle Mountain

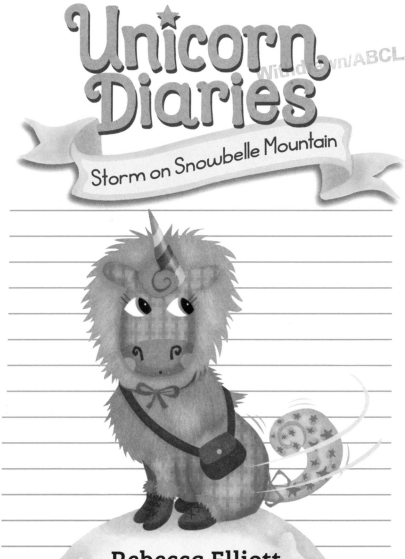

Rebecca Elliott

SCHOLASTIC INC.

For my agent, Laetitia, who has
helped me weather a few storms. —R.E.

The publisher does not have any control over and does not assume
any responsibility for author or third-party websites or their content.

No part of this publication may be reproduced, stored in a retrieval system,
or transmitted in any form or by any means, electronic, mechanical,
photocopying, recording, or otherwise, without written permission of the
publisher. For information regarding permission, write to Scholastic Inc.,
Attention: Permissions Department, 557 Broadway, New York, NY 10012.

This book is a work of fiction. Names, characters, places, and incidents are
either the product of the author's imagination or are used fictitiously, and any
resemblance to actual persons, living or dead, business establishments,
events, or locales is entirely coincidental.

Library of Congress Cataloging-in-Publication Data

Names: Elliott, Rebecca, author, illustrator. | Elliott, Rebecca. Unicorn diaries ; 6.
Title: Storm on Snowbelle Mountain / Rebecca Elliott.
Description: First edition. | New York : Branches/Scholastic Inc., 2022. |
Series: Unicorn diaries ; 6 | Summary: Despite disagreements on the wisdom of the
adventure, Rainbow Tinseltail and the other unicorns set out for Snowbelle Mountain
to find out if Yetis are real—and when they get caught in a blizzard and
take shelter in a cave they find the answer to their quest.
Identifiers: LCCN 2021001198 | ISBN 9781338745627 (paperback) |
ISBN 9781338745634 (hardcover) | ISBN 9781338745641 (ebk)
Subjects: LCSH: Unicorns—Juvenile fiction. | Yeti—Juvenile fiction. |
Blizzard—Juvenile fiction. | Friendship—Juvenile fiction. |
CYAC: Unicorns—Fiction. | Yeti—Fiction. |
Blizzards—Fiction. | Friendship—Fiction. | Diaries—Fiction.
Classification: LCC PZ7.E45812 St 2022 | DDC [Fic]—dc23
LC record available at https://lccn.loc.gov/2021001198

10 9 8 7 6 5 4 3 2 1   22 23 24 25 26

Printed in China 62
First edition, January 2022

Book design by Marissa Asuncion

Table of Contents

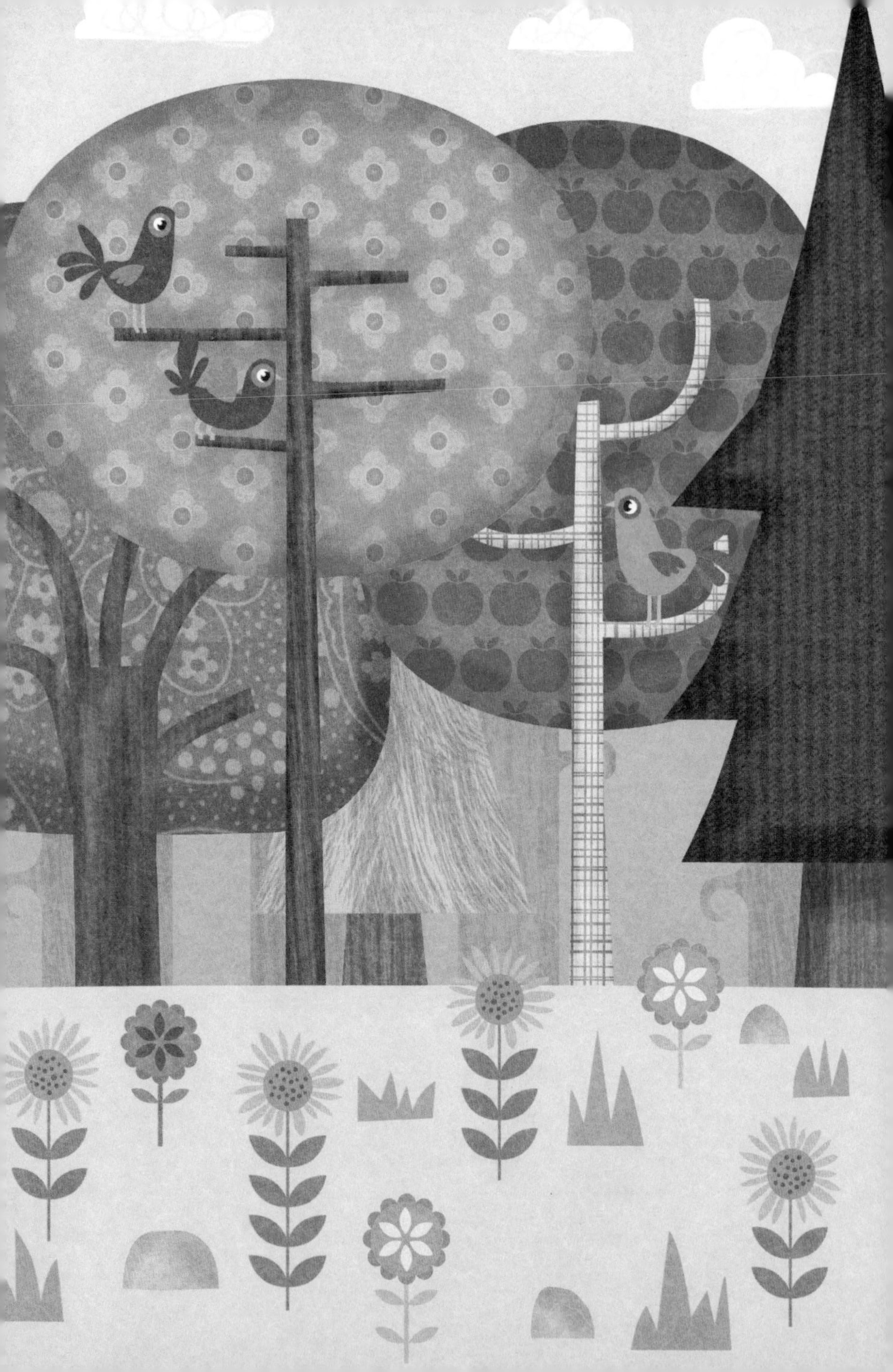

Look, It's a Rainbow!

Sunday

Hello again, Diary! It's me, Bo! (Short for Rainbow Tinseltail.) I'm ready for another adventure in Sparklegrove Forest.

Here's a map of the forest and all its magical places:

Rainbow Falls

Troll Caves

Glimmer Glade

Sparklegrove School for Unicorns

Dragon Nests

Budbloom Meadow

Snowbelle Mountain

Unipods

Goldie's
Cave

Fairy Village

Twinkleplop
Lagoon

Goblin
Castle

Lots of magical creatures live
here, including . . .

Yetis! I'm not sure if they exist or not.
But if they do, this is what we know
about them:

They are also
known as abominable
snowmen. (Don't they
sound scary?!)

They live high
up on Snowbelle
Mountain.

No one living
in Sparklegrove
Forest has ever
actually seen them.

They are big and
hairy. And their fur
blends in with the snow!

We unicorns are very easy to spot in the snow since we're brightly colored!

Tail
Fun to braid, and swishing it makes our Unicorn Powers work.

Horn
Good for scratching one another's backs.

Legs
Good for galloping super fast.

Nose
Very good at smelling. My favorite smells are cut grass and cloud fluff pie.

Here are more fun unicorn facts:

We live together in **UNIPODS**.

We glow when we're nervous.

Our manes smell like strawberries.

We sleep on cloud beds.

Sparklegrove School for Unicorns is the best school. It's also my home!

My friends all have different Unicorn Powers. I'm a Wish Unicorn.

I can grant one wish every week.

This is Sunny Huckleberry. He's my BEST friend, and he can turn invisible whenever he wants to, which is cool!

Here is everyone else at my school and all their magical powers.

Nutmeg Silvertips
Flying Unicorn

Scarlett Sugarlumps
Thingamabob Unicorn

Jed Glitterock
Weather Unicorn

Monty Dumpling
Size-Changer Unicorn

Piper Forestine
Healer Unicorn

Mr. Rumptwinkle
Shape-Shifter Unicorn

At S.S.U., we have all kinds of **TWINKLE-TASTIC** lessons, like:

MAGICAL CHEMISTRY

EXPLORERS OF
SPARKLEGROVE FOREST

HORN ART

GYM

Unicorns each have a special patch blanket. Every week we learn or do something new to earn our next patch.

I can't wait to hear what patch our teacher, Mr. Rumptwinkle, says we're working toward this week! Good night, Diary!

2

Let's Go Exploring!

Monday

Before school this morning, we baked my favorite SNURPLEBERRY MUFFINS.

We normally all eat breakfast together, but when we sat down, three unicorns were missing.

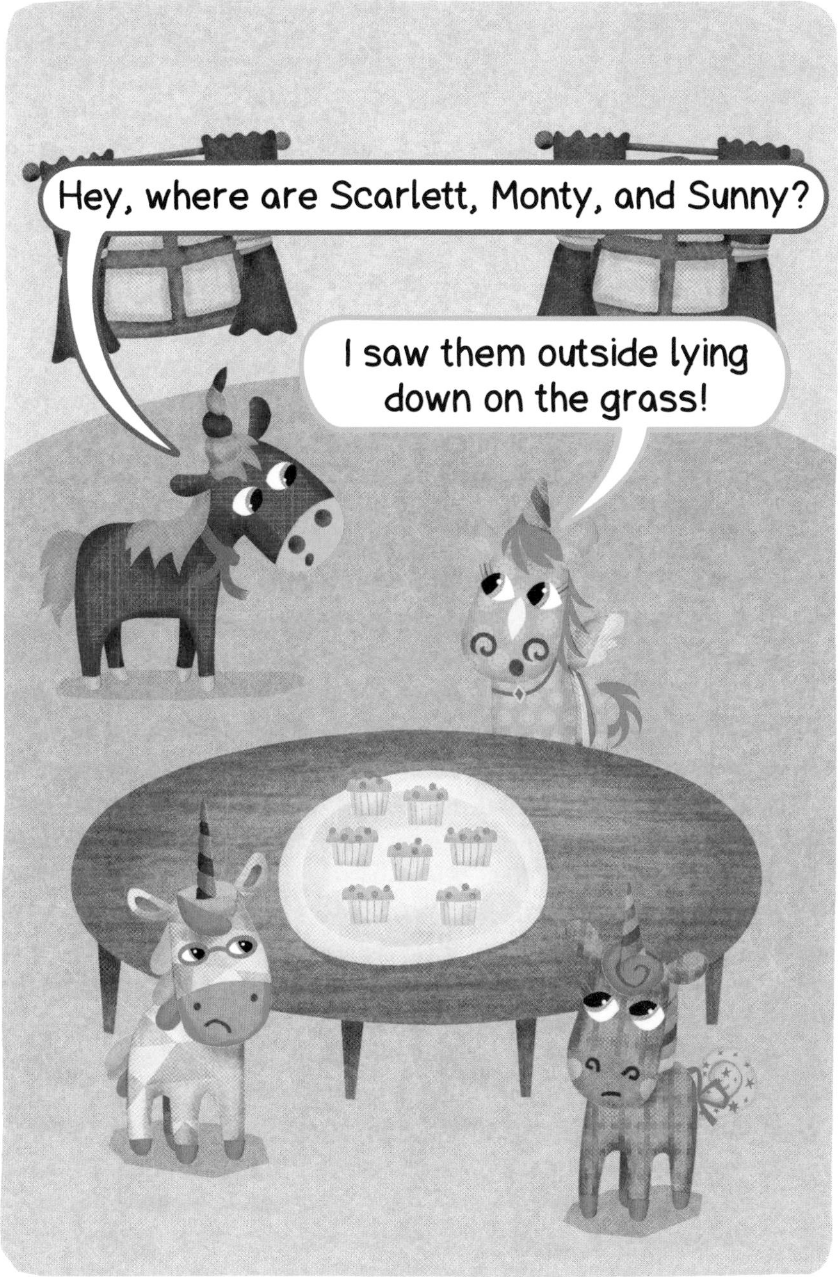
Hey, where are Scarlett, Monty, and Sunny?
I saw them outside lying down on the grass!

We went outside to find them.

The clouds _did_ look amazing. But I was worried that we'd be late for school!

We had breakfast, which we all agreed was really yummy.

Then, we trotted along to our first EXPLORERS OF SPARKLEGROVE FOREST lesson with Mr. Rumptwinkle.

We learned all about explorers like Sir Edmund Hornbury, who set out to find a yeti.

He was super brave! And for years, he searched for yetis on top of Snowbelle Mountain.

Did he prove they exist?

Of course not. Yetis aren't real!

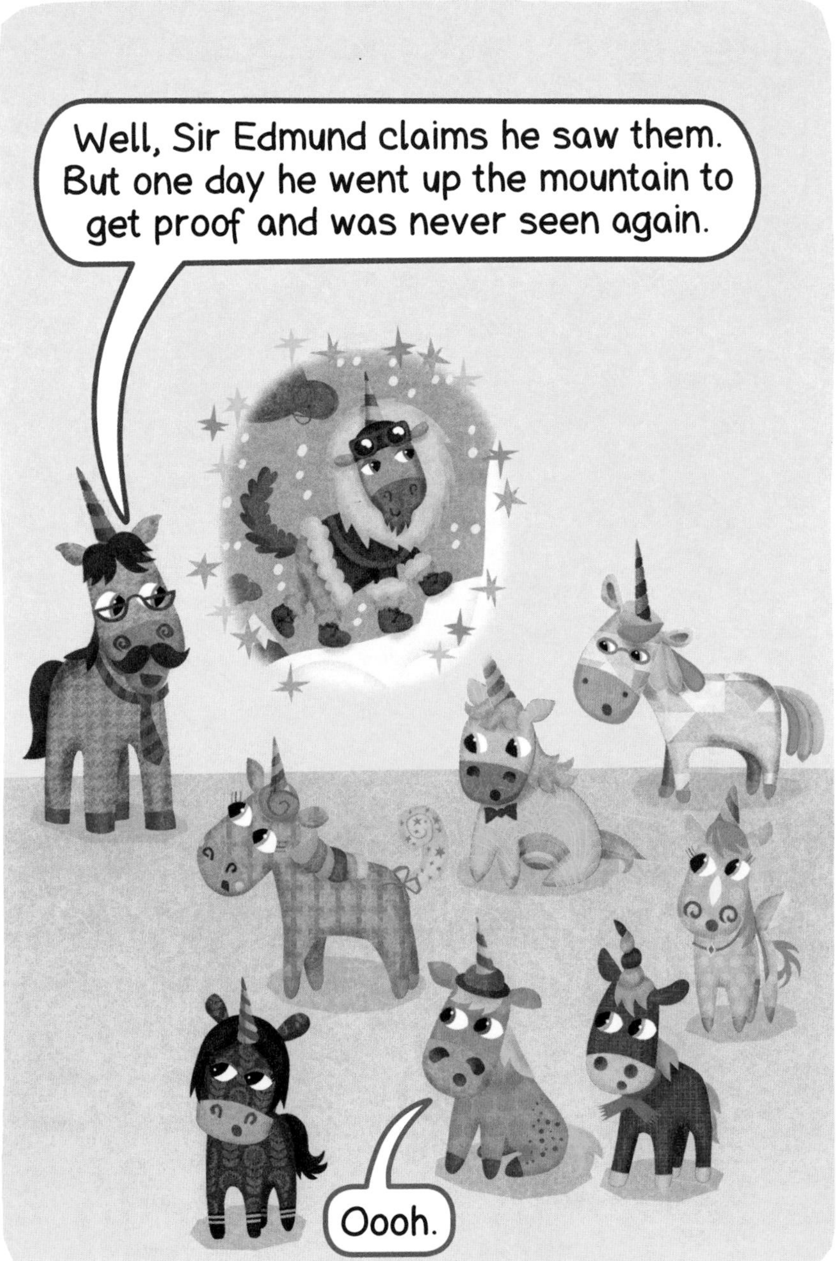
Well, Sir Edmund claims he saw them. But one day he went up the mountain to get proof and was never seen again.
Oooh.

We were all eager to hear which patch we'd earn this week at Friday's Patch Parade.

How do we get it?

Tomorrow, you will go camping on Snowbelle Mountain all on your own. You need to explore the mountain, looking for the best place to ski!

After school, we galloped to our **UNIPODS** and started packing. I picked my warmest clothes, including my favorite fluffy hoof warmers and my best skis.

I couldn't wait for our adventure to begin, but I was also a little bit scared.

I felt better knowing that Sunny wasn't worried. But Sunny doesn't really worry about anything . . . Wish me luck, Diary!

3

The Blizzard

Tuesday

My friends and I set off up the mountain nice and early.

We trotted halfway up the mountain to where we normally ski.

Should we do some skiing here?

Maybe we should go a bit higher, since we're trying to earn our EXPLORER patch?

I wasn't sure it was a good idea. There were a few dark clouds in the sky.

Higher sounds exciting!

Yeah! I feel like Sir Edmund Hornbury!

Jed, Piper, and Nutmeg looked worried, too. But it did look exciting farther up the mountain. There was more snow and I could see fun jumps to ski over. . . So we all agreed.

When we got really high up, we started to ski. It was **GLITTERRIFIC** fun!

And then – DISASTER! A big storm started!

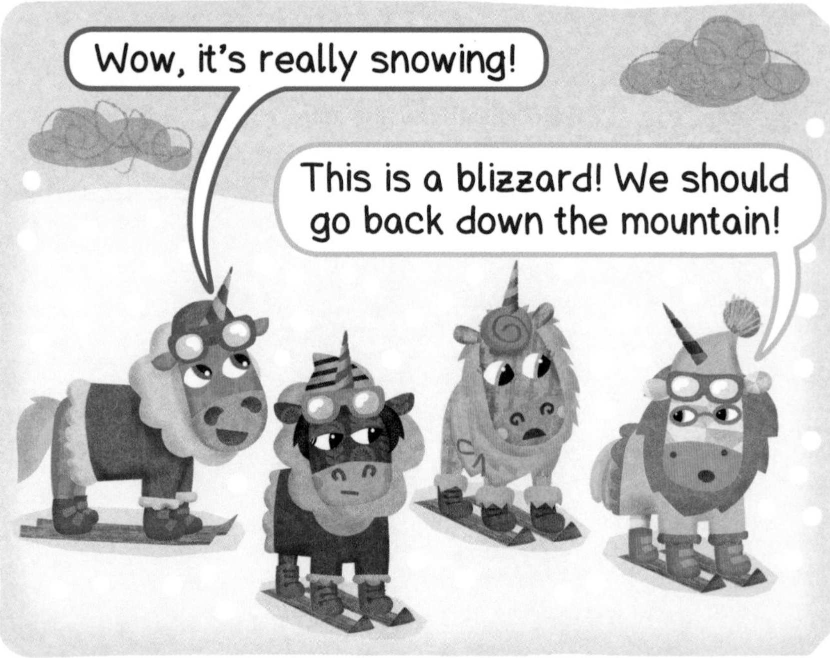
Wow, it's really snowing!
This is a blizzard! We should go back down the mountain!

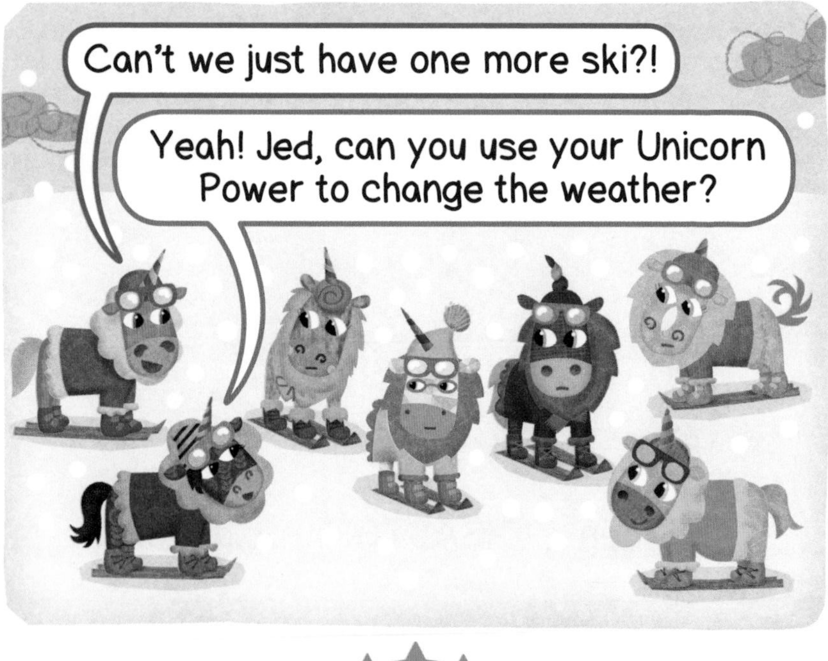
Can't we just have one more ski?!
Yeah! Jed, can you use your Unicorn Power to change the weather?

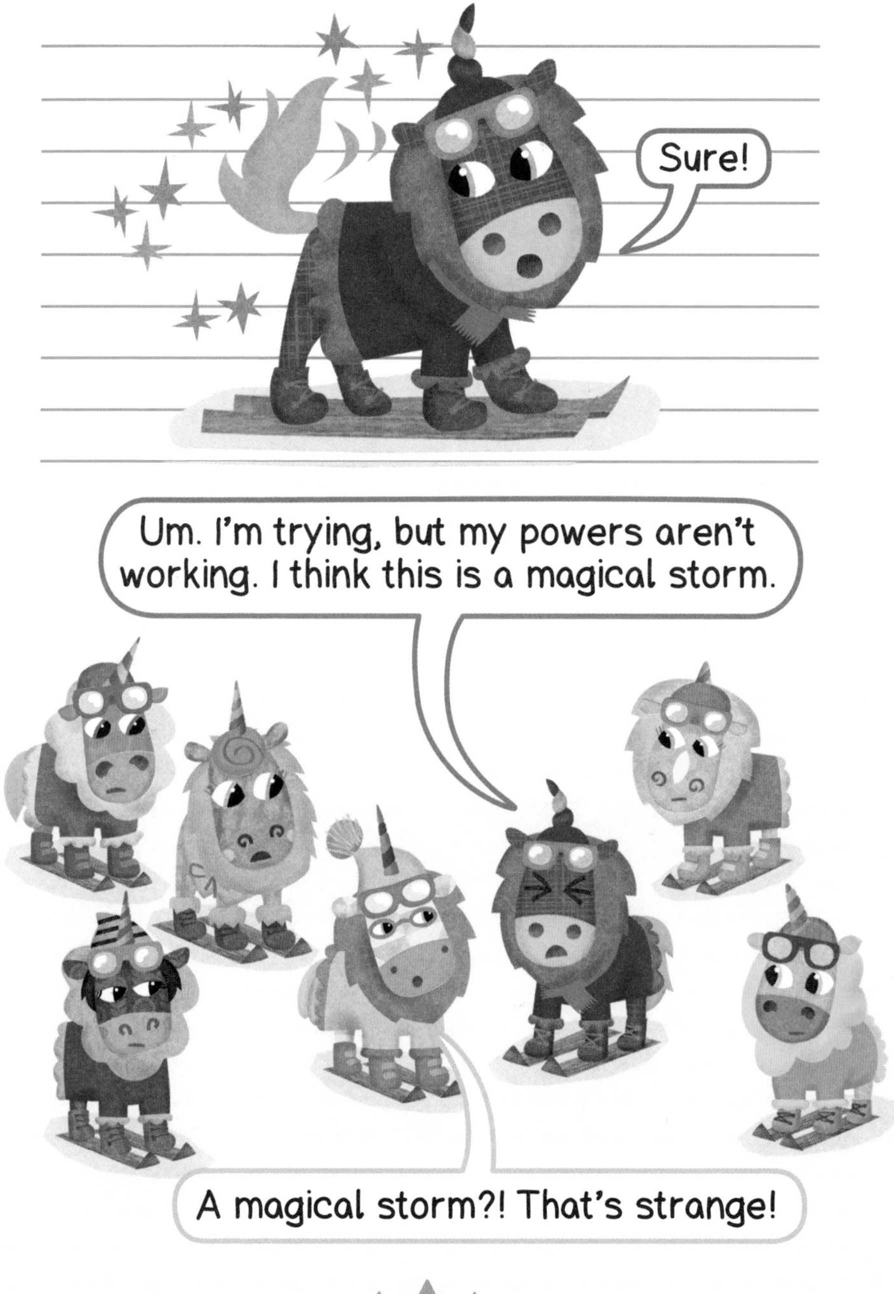
Sure!
Um. I'm trying, but my powers aren't working. I think this is a magical storm.
A magical storm?! That's strange!

Piper, Jed, Nutmeg, and I wanted to leave before the storm got too bad. But Sunny, Monty, and Scarlett wanted to keep skiing.

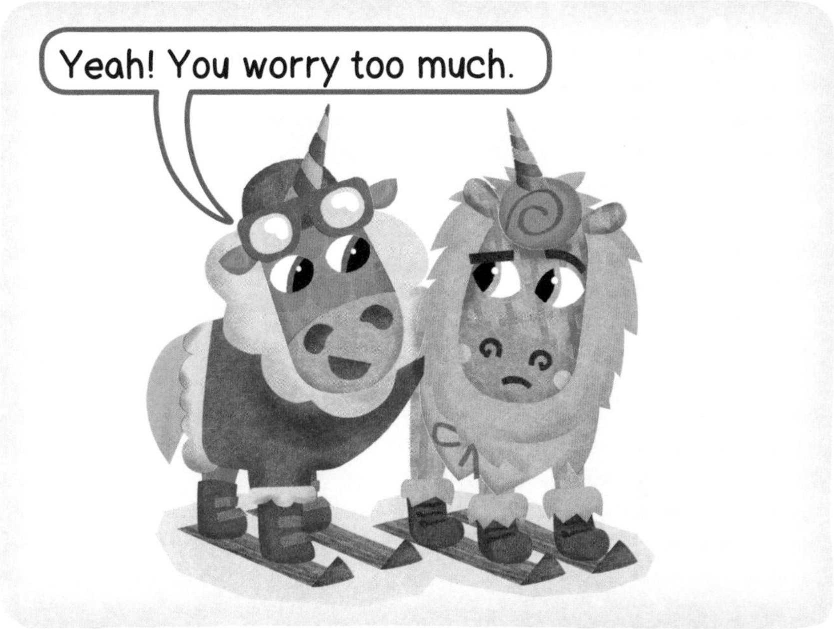
Yeah! You worry too much.

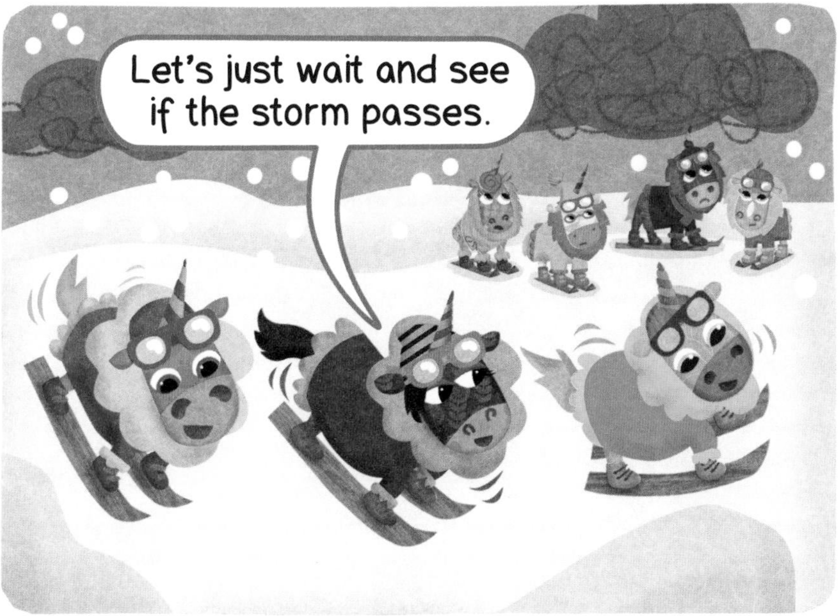
Let's just wait and see if the storm passes.

But the storm didn't go away. Jed was right. IT GOT WORSE! Before long, it was really windy and we could hardly see.

We galloped higher up the mountain, but we couldn't find anywhere!

I swished my tail to make Piper's wish come true.

We could see little glowing insects!

We followed the fireflies and they led us to a cave. The wish had worked!

We settled into our sleeping bags and drank warm **MOON SOUP**. It made us feel all warm and snuggly.

We were super tired but it was difficult to sleep with the storm howling around outside.

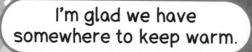

I'm glad we have somewhere to keep warm.

I knew we'd be all right, Bo.

As long as the yetis don't get us!

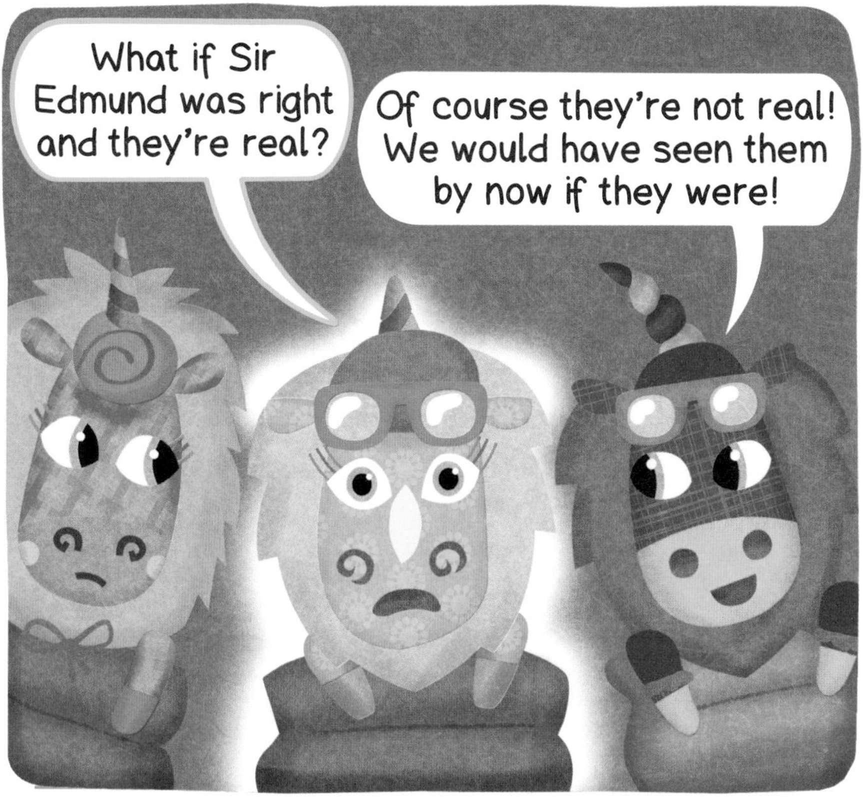
What if Sir Edmund was right and they're real?
Of course they're not real! We would have seen them by now if they were!

I wasn't too worried about yetis, but I was worried about the storm. The truth is, Diary, I was a little upset with Sunny, Monty, and Scarlett for not listening when we said that we should go back down the mountain. But I didn't say anything because Sunny is my best friend. Well, that and because I was tired after climbing this huge mountain . . .

4
The Missing Unicorns

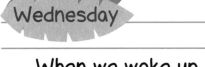
Wednesday

When we woke up, it was still dark and snowing. But it seemed like the worst of the storm had passed.

The storm is going! Yay!

Jed looked worried though.

My weather powers are telling me the storm could pick back up at any moment.

Oooh. We should hurry back down the mountain, then.

Let's pack everything up and get going.

Piper, Jed, Nutmeg, and I thought it was better if we left right away. But our other three friends wanted to stay and watch the sunrise first.

Come on. We need to go!

But look at this sunrise. Isn't it <u>sparkle-tastic</u>?!

It would look even better from higher up the mountain. Let's climb!

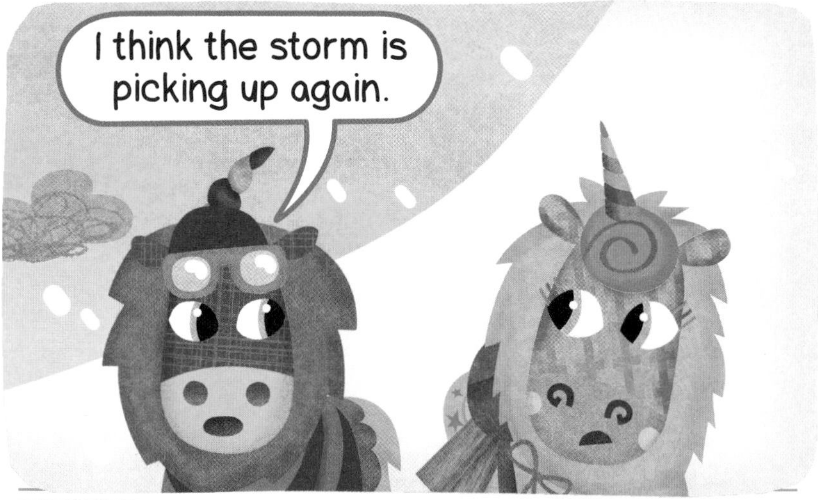

I think the storm is picking up again.

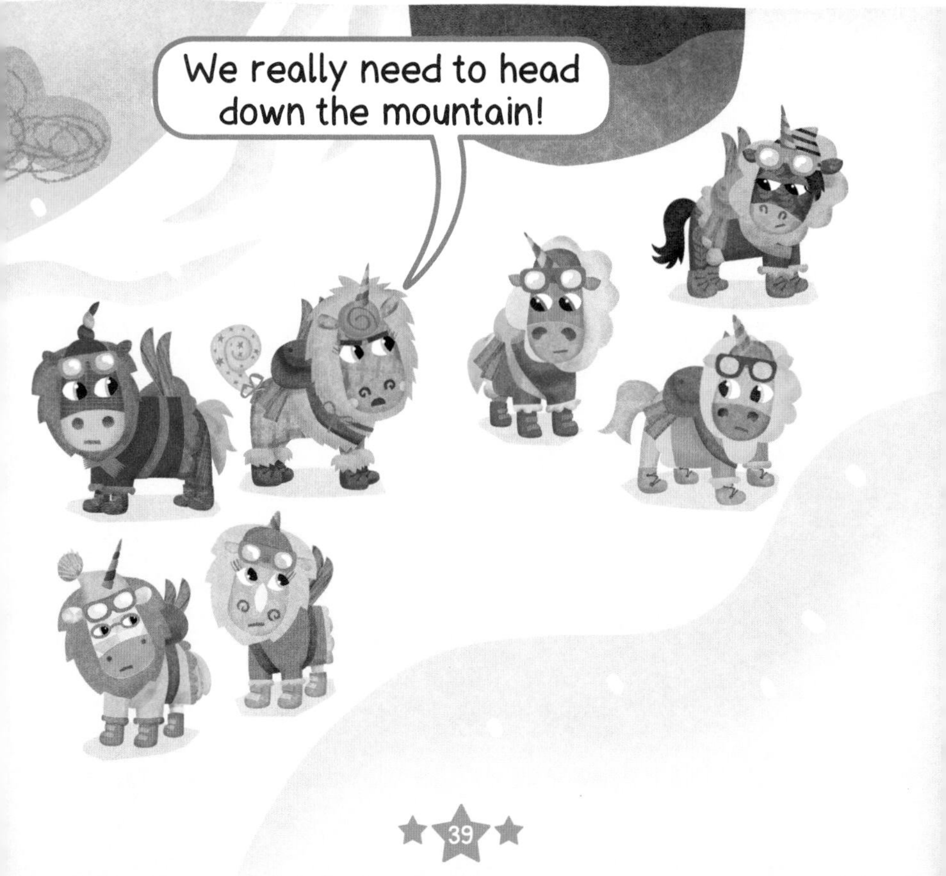

We really need to head down the mountain!

I was more than a little bit upset now. I was feeling mad!

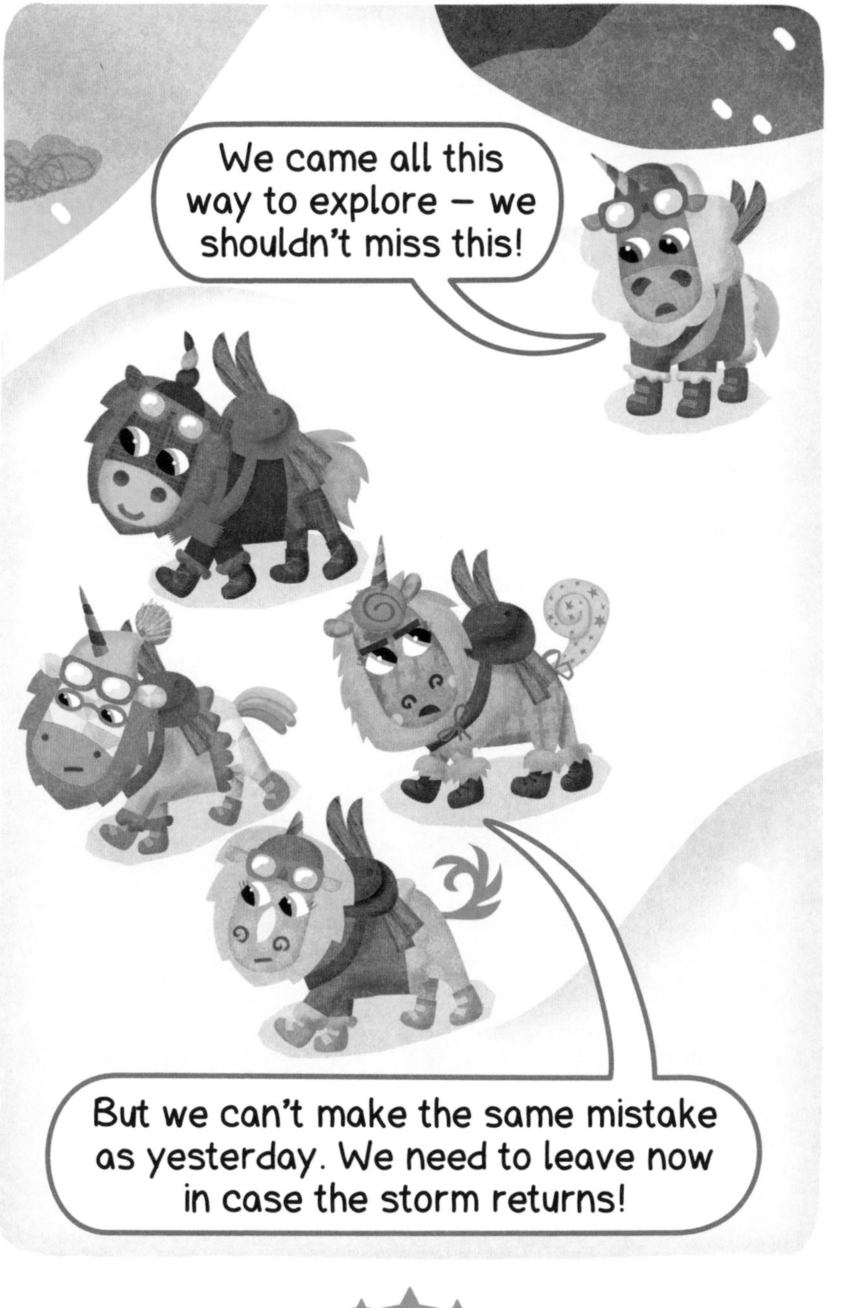
We came all this way to explore – we shouldn't miss this!
But we can't make the same mistake as yesterday. We need to leave now in case the storm returns!

It took us all day to make it down the mountain. The wind and snow had picked up again, so we could hardly see one another! Finally, we made it back to our UNIPOD. We were so happy to see Mr. Rumptwinkle waiting for us!

We had a big adventure!

That's great! But . . . where are Monty and Scarlett?

We turned around and realized they weren't with us!!

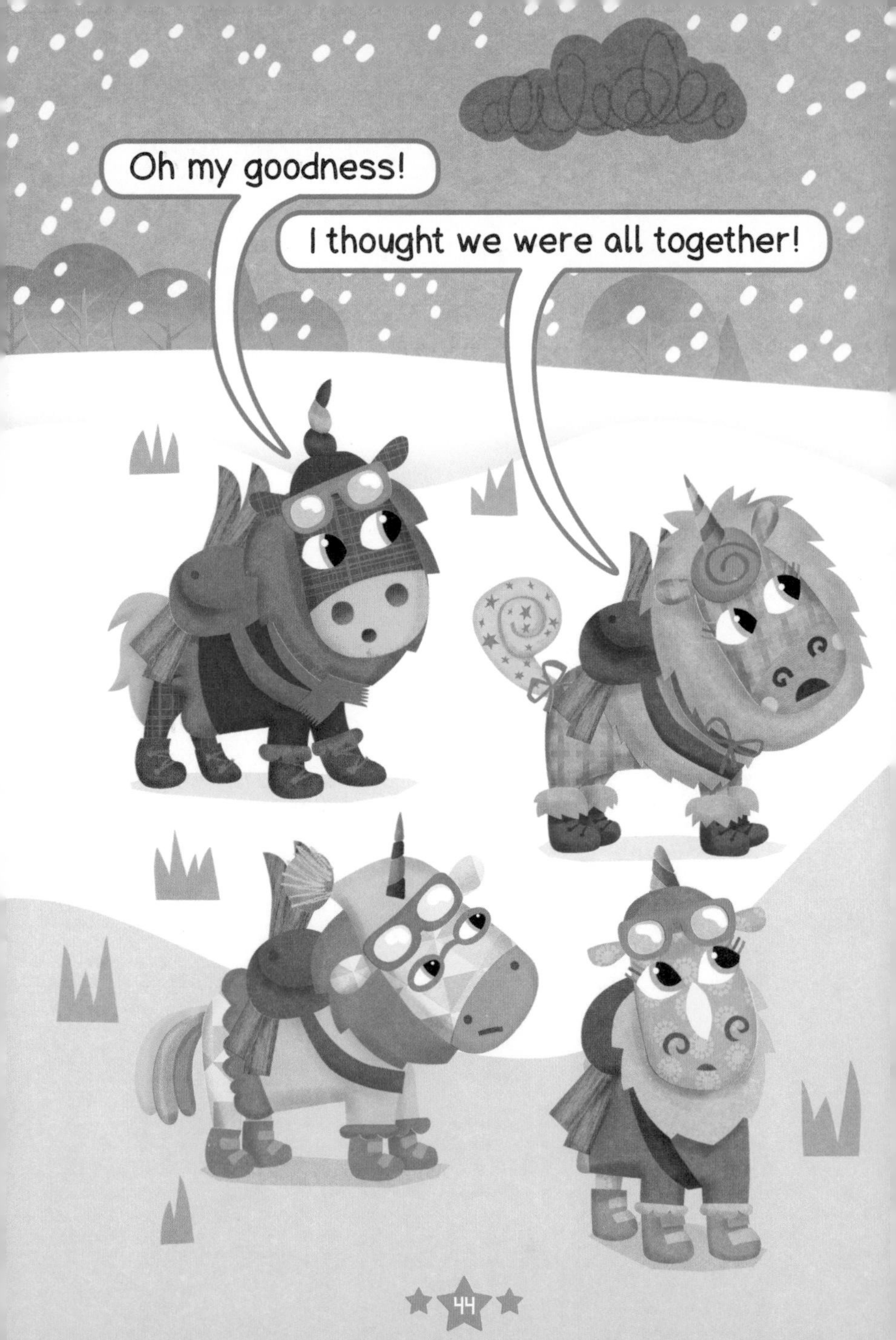
Oh my goodness!
I thought we were all together!

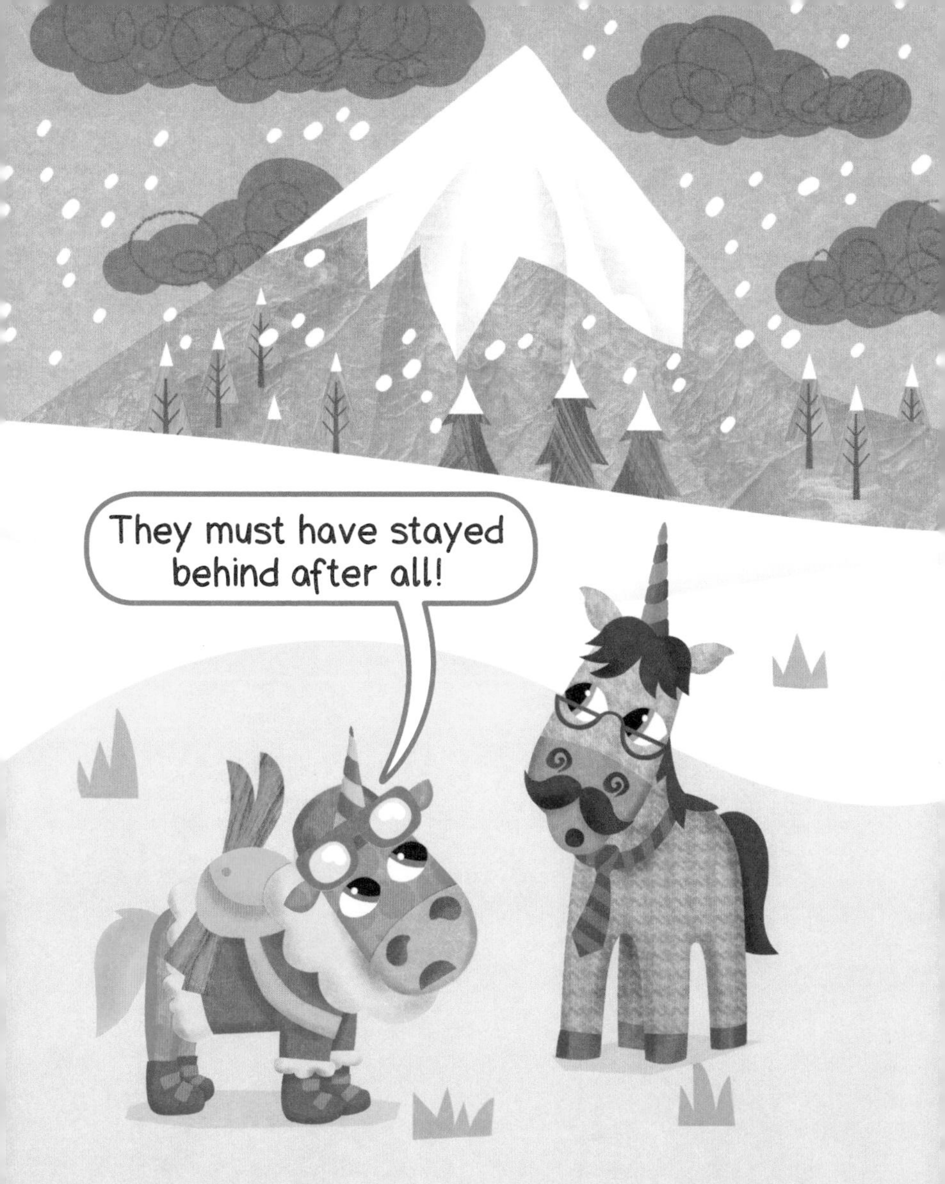
They must have stayed behind after all!

Oh Diary, I was so worried about them being stuck up there in this storm!

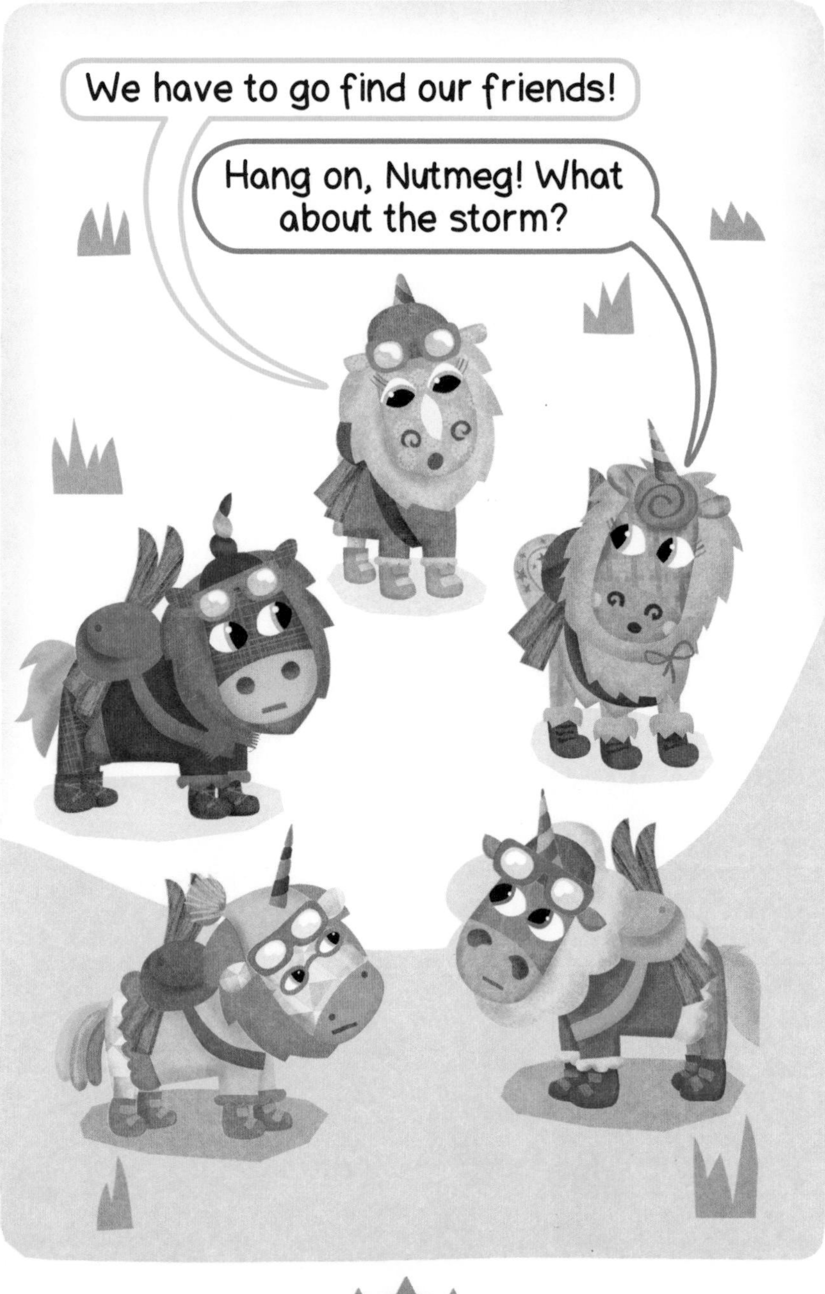
We have to go find our friends!
Hang on, Nutmeg! What about the storm?

So we went to sleep, but we were super worried about our friends. We hoped we'd find them up on the mountain tomorrow.

5

An Abominable Discovery

Thursday

We left for Snowbelle Mountain as soon as the sun came up.

I'm glad it has stopped snowing.

At least for now. But those clouds over the mountain look very dark.

We trotted along all day. Feeling cold and tired, we finally got to the cave. We rushed inside!

But Scarlett and Monty weren't there.

We wanted to keep searching for them, but our **HOOVES** were too cold.

We were just about to leave the cave when Nutmeg noticed something.

Now we knew where to find them!

As we climbed the mountain, the clouds got super dark. Even with our horns glowing, we could hardly see one another.

Suddenly, we heard a loud thudding sound.

THUD!! THUD!!

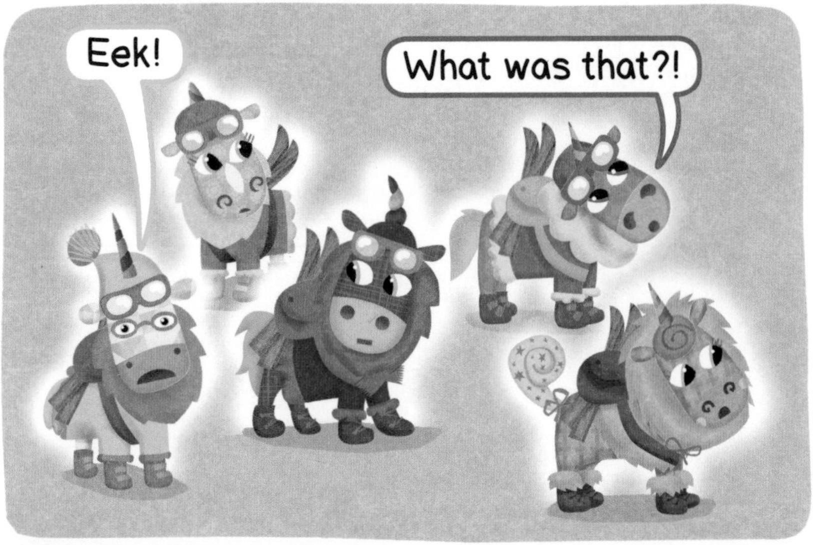
Eek!
What was that?!

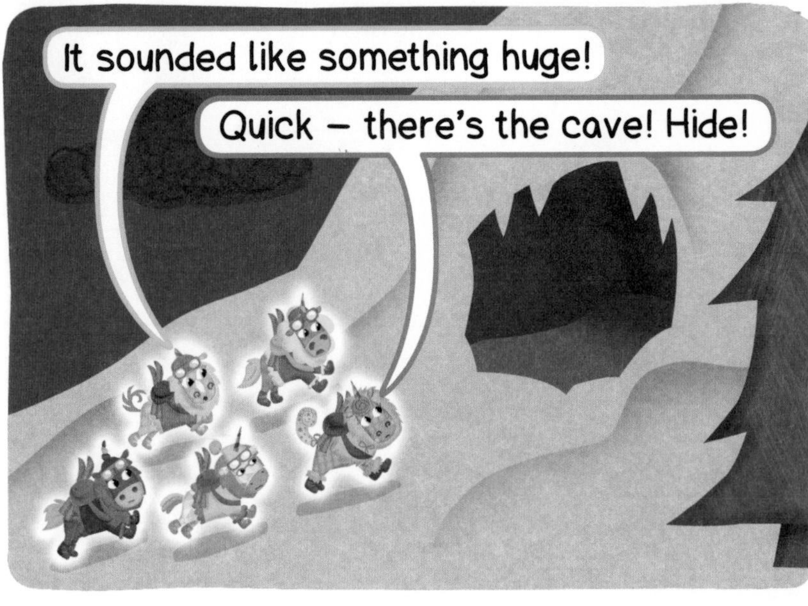
It sounded like something huge!
Quick – there's the cave! Hide!

But when we got inside, we realized the creatures making those huge sounds were INSIDE the cave!

Diary, we were so scared! But then we heard our friends' voices.

We were so happy to find our friends safe and warm. We all had a big unicorn group hug.

Then, one of the yetis put his big, furry arms around all of us. He spoke in a really gentle voice.

That's it. Hug it out, little uni-dudes.

But you're . . . you're YETIS!

We thought you weren't real!

We thought you were scary!

Hey, just chill. We're cool.

And we're real! And real friendly, too.

It's true. They are!

The yetis introduced themselves.

As we all sat around eating snow cones together, I spotted a picture on the wall.

Is that Sir Edmund Hornbury?

It totally is Sir Eddy. He chilled with us for years.
Then he went off on a new adventure to find the Loch Ness Monster.
Wow! So Sir Edmund did see yetis. He even had proof — that picture!
So why didn't he show it to anyone?

Sir Eddy realized he didn't want to rush around and prove something just to be famous.

Instead, he was happy just hanging out with us, snow-surfing and watching the sunsets. Ha.

Sometimes, you just gotta chill.

I thought about how Sunny, Scarlett, and Monty were always stopping to look at clouds and sunsets instead of getting stuff done. Maybe they had the right idea sometimes.

The wind was getting strong again. We could hear it blowing the snow around the mountain outside the cave.

Surf's up, dude!
Want to catch some snow-waves with us?
You bet!
Let's hit the slopes!

The yetis let us ride on their snow surfboards. We had the most SNOW-TASTIC time surfing the snow-waves!

When it got dark, we went to the yetis' cave. They played us cool music on their guitars to help us sleep.

Sunny, I'm happy you're so laid-back. Don't ever stop looking at the sunrise.

Thanks, Bo. And I'm happy you get things done — you're awesome.

6

Surf's Up!

We slept so well after surfing that we ended up sleeping in really late!

We all looked at Dylan and Harley at the same time.

Surf's up!

Then we surfed down the mountain.

When we got home, Mr. Rumptwinkle was waiting for us. We kept the yetis hidden in the snow.

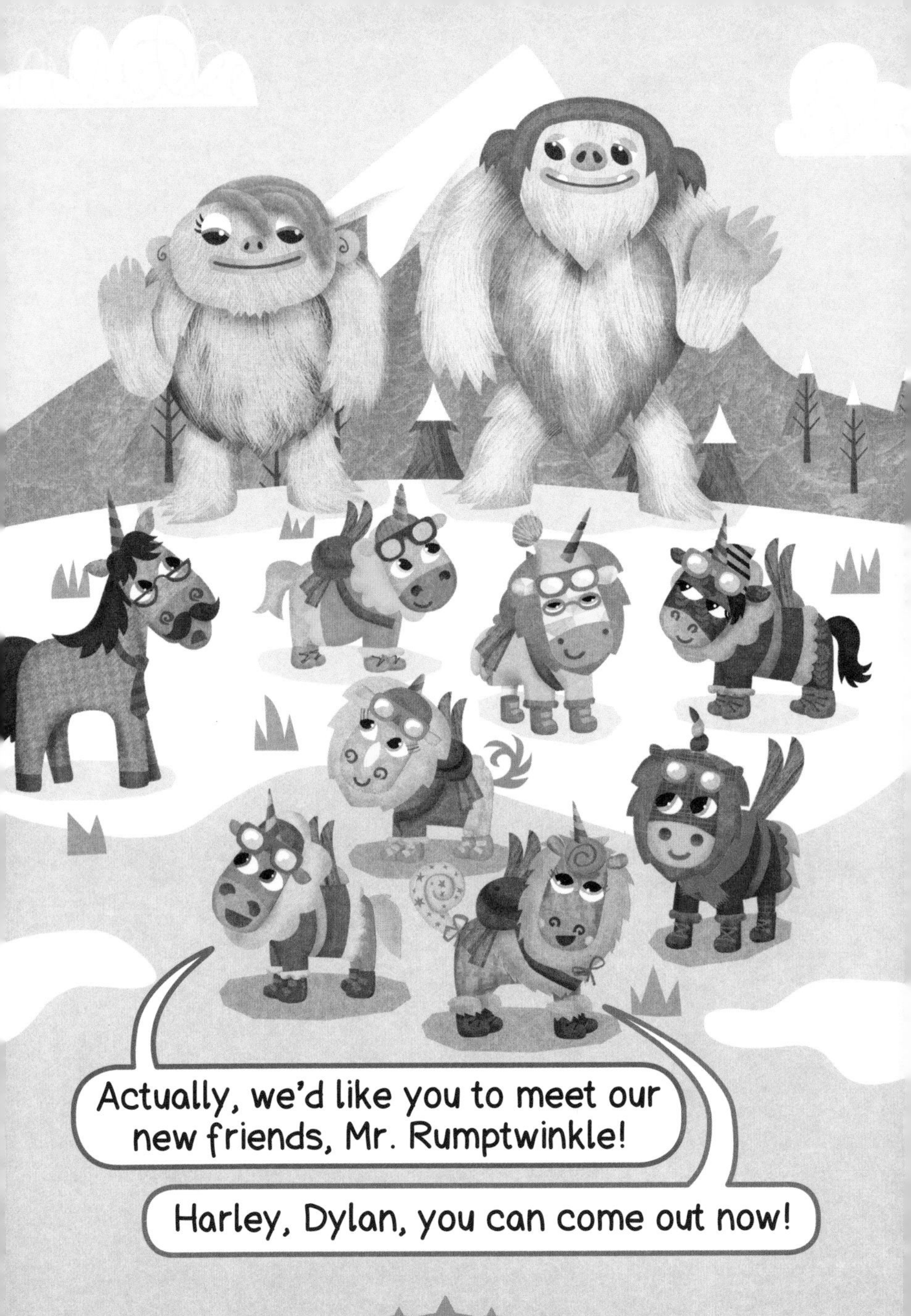
Actually, we'd like you to meet our new friends, Mr. Rumptwinkle!
Harley, Dylan, you can come out now!

The yetis came forward to shake Mr. Rumptwinkle's hoof. He was in so much shock, he shape-shifted about five times!

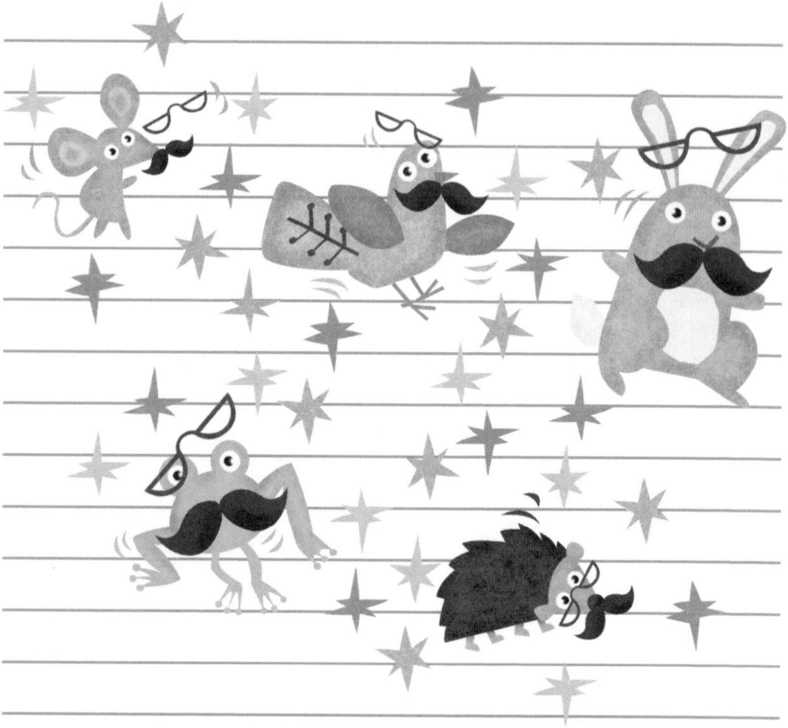

But then our teacher couldn't stop smiling!

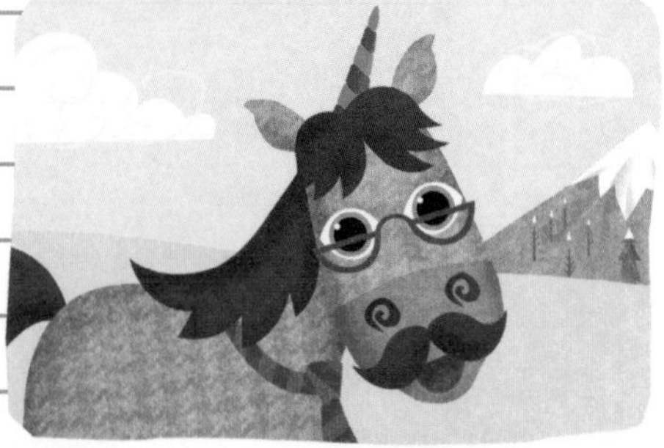

Sparkles swirled around us.

Then, we ate more snow cones and partied all night!

7

Chillax Time!

Diary, can you believe we stayed up ALL NIGHT long?!

It's so late, the sun is coming up! Do you think we should go to sleep now?

Oh Sunny, you should just relax some more. We've got time to watch the sunrise first!

We lay back in the snow and watched the sunrise. It was beautiful.

I'm super tired, but happy. I think I'll just lie back here and do nothing for a while — because sometimes that's okay! See you next time!

Rebecca Elliott may not have a magical horn or sneeze glitter, but she's still a lot like a unicorn. Rebecca always tries to have a positive attitude, she likes to laugh a lot, and she lives with some great creatures — her noisy-yet-charming children, her lovable but naughty dog Frida, and a big, lazy cat named Bernard. She gets to hang out with these fun characters and write stories for a living, so she thinks her life is pretty magical!

Rebecca is the author of several picture books, the young adult novel PRETTY FUNNY FOR A GIRL, the bestselling Unicorn Diaries early chapter book series, and the bestselling Owl Diaries series.

Unicorn Diaries

How much do you know about Storm on Snowbelle Mountain?

What are some facts about yetis?

How did the unicorns earn their EXPLORER patches?

What did Sir Edmund Hornbury set out to do? Did his goal change? Reread Chapters 2 and 5.

Think about a time you and a friend disagreed about the right way to do something. Why do you think they felt their way was best?

Draw a postcard of a place you'd like to explore!